The Moving-Box Sukkah

By Leah Rachel Berkowitz · Illustrated by Sharon Vargo

APPLES & HONEY PRESS

To Miles: Tsads built a sukkah for me.
Tante wrote this book for you.
—LRB

To my parents,
who showed me the stars.
—SV

The illustrations in this book were created by Sharon Vargo with a combination of traditional and digital media.

Apples & Honey Press
An Imprint of Behrman House Publishers
Millburn, New Jersey 07041
www.applesandhoneypress.com

ISBN 978-1-68115-627-9

Library of Congress Catalog Number: 2022056162

Design by Elynn Cohen
Art direction by Ann D. Koffsky
Edited by Dena Neusner
Printed in China

9 8 7 6 5 4 3 2 1

0924/B2627/A5

Mom and I just moved to the city, and everything is different here. Even the bus to school is a different color.

Each time we unpack a box, I look for my blue blanket, the one I've had since I was little. I'm worried it's still in our old house. Sometimes I wish I was still in our old house too.

I can't see the trees changing color from up here on the seventeenth floor. All I can see are other windows. But I know the leaves are changing down below, which means it's almost time for Sukkot.

"Where will we build a sukkah this year?" I ask Mom.
"We don't even have a yard!"

Mom and I used to invite our neighbors over for dinner in our sukkah. Some nights we'd even camp out under the stars. How will we do that now?

"We'll think of something," Mom says.
"What do we need to make a sukkah?"

I tell her that a sukkah has at least three walls. And a roof made of branches to let the stars shine through.

Coats

Mom reaches into a box and pulls out our jackets, like a magic trick. "There's a park around the corner," she says. "Maybe we can find some branches there."

I peek inside the box. No blue blanket.

The trees lining the sidewalk are scattered and scrawny. But when we turn the corner, it's as if we've landed on another planet. The trees are bursting with color, from bright greens to fiery reds and oranges.

All I can say is, "Wow."

Mom winks at me. "Maybe the city's not so bad after all?"

I take off running. It feels good to be outside.

Mom and I gather fallen branches. "You know," she says, "the seventeenth floor isn't the strangest place to build a sukkah."

"What do you mean?"

"There's an old story that, long ago, a rabbi tried to build
a sukkah on a boat," Mom says. "But the wind blew it over."

"No way!" I say.

"Another time, someone built a sukkah on a camel," she says. "But it was too tall for anyone to climb inside."

"And too bumpy to eat in!" I add.

"You'll never guess what they tried next." Mom drops her voice to a whisper. "They used an elephant as a sukkah wall!"

"But what if it ran away?" I laugh. "Then they'd have no sukkah at all!"

"And a runaway elephant!" Mom says.

"Do you know why I like these stories?" Mom asks.

I shake my head.

"They remind me that our people have moved around a lot, ever since the ancient Israelites left Egypt. Wherever they went, they had to figure out how to celebrate the holidays all over again."

"Just like us?" I ask.

Mom nods. "Just like us."

I look at our pile of twigs and branches, imagining how they'd look against the night sky. "Now we have our roof, but what can we use for walls?"

"I don't know," Mom says. "All those boxes, and I forgot to pack an elephant!"

"That's it!" I scramble to my feet. "We can use the moving boxes!"

Mom helps me carry the branches back to our apartment.

We stack the boxes to make three cardboard walls.

We crisscross twigs and branches over the top and spread out our sleeping bags underneath.

Toys

It feels cozy lying in our moving-box sukkah. But I still wish we were in our old backyard.

"Mom?" I ask. "When will this feel like home?"

"It might take a while," Mom says. "You know, the Israelites wandered in the wilderness for forty years."

"That must have felt like forever!" I say.

"But they'd look up at night and see the same stars they'd always seen. That was all they needed to make the wilderness feel like home."

I gaze up at the twigs and branches, wishing I was looking up at the night sky.

Then I close my eyes,
and I see it—
a sky full of stars.

I imagine us camping
in the desert...

standing on the deck
of a ship...

riding on the back
of a camel . . .

setting our table next
to an elephant . . .

lying in the grass
behind our old house.

Suddenly, my feet brush against something soft in my sleeping bag.

"My blanket!" I hug it close to my heart. It smells like cut grass and clean laundry, like picnics in our old backyard. It smells like home.

"I knew it would turn up," Mom says.

I trace the faded pattern with my fingertips. "The stars are still the same."

"Even here?" Mom asks.

"Even here."

And that gives me an idea.

With my blanket spread over the top of our sukkah,
it looks like we're underneath a starry night sky.

I snuggle close to Mom. Lots of things still feel new
and different. But as long as we're together, we have
everything we need to make this place feel like home.

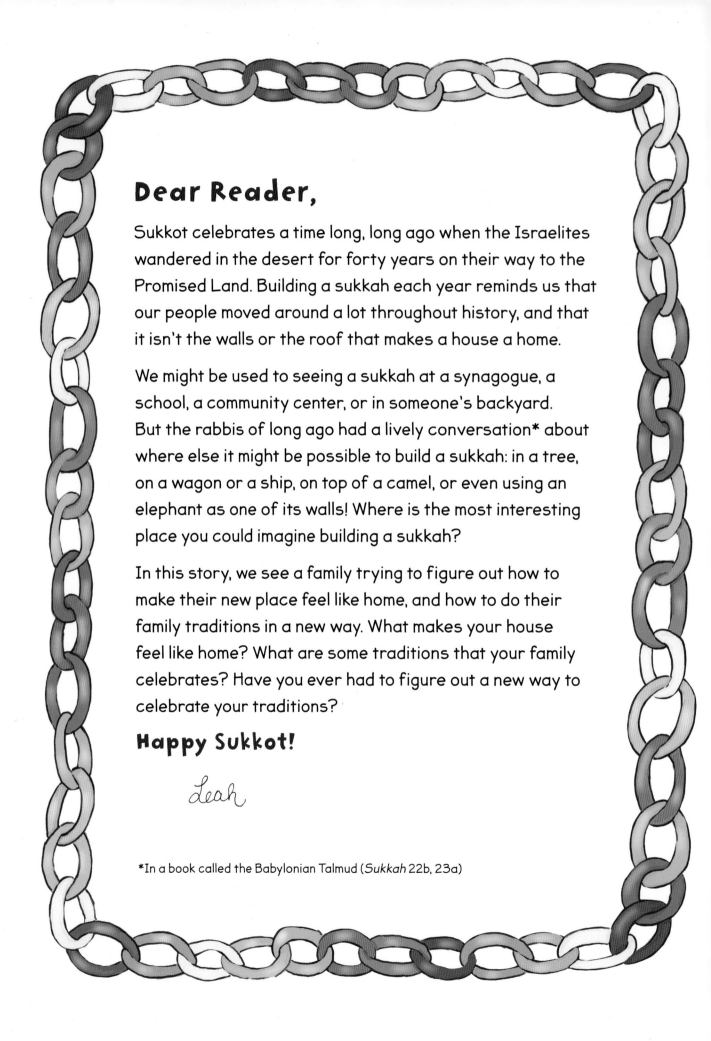

Dear Reader,

Sukkot celebrates a time long, long ago when the Israelites wandered in the desert for forty years on their way to the Promised Land. Building a sukkah each year reminds us that our people moved around a lot throughout history, and that it isn't the walls or the roof that makes a house a home.

We might be used to seeing a sukkah at a synagogue, a school, a community center, or in someone's backyard. But the rabbis of long ago had a lively conversation* about where else it might be possible to build a sukkah: in a tree, on a wagon or a ship, on top of a camel, or even using an elephant as one of its walls! Where is the most interesting place you could imagine building a sukkah?

In this story, we see a family trying to figure out how to make their new place feel like home, and how to do their family traditions in a new way. What makes your house feel like home? What are some traditions that your family celebrates? Have you ever had to figure out a new way to celebrate your traditions?

Happy Sukkot!

Leah

*In a book called the Babylonian Talmud (*Sukkah* 22b, 23a)